From Malaika (May 23) :j

The Cat's Tale

by Lynne Rickards and Karl West

W
FRANKLIN WATTS
LONDON•SYDNEY

Long ago, in China,

there lived an emperor.

He wanted to count the years to see

how old he was.

"If I give every New Year a name,

I can count them," he said.

Then, the Emperor had an idea.

"I will give each New Year the name

of an animal," he said.

"The animals must have a race.

The first twelve animals to swim across

the river will be the winners."

So the Emperor called all the animals

and told them about the swimming race.

Cat was not happy.

She did not like to swim.

"I don't like water!" she said to Rat.
"But I want to win the race
and give the New Year my name."

"I want to give the New Year my name," Rat said to himself. "I need a plan to help me win the race."

After a while, he smiled.

"I have a plan," said Rat to Cat.

"Ox can swim fast. Let's ride on his back.

When he gets near the bank,

we will jump off."

"Yes, that is a good plan," said Cat.

"We will win the race."

Cat and Rat went to see Ox.

"Please, Ox," said Rat,
"my friend Cat does not like to swim.
Can you help her across the river?"

"Yes, I will help you," Ox said to Cat.

It was the day of the race.

All the animals lined up

along the river bank.

"Ready, steady, go!" said the Emperor,

and in jumped the animals.

Cat and Rat looked at Ox.

Now it was time for their plan.

Cat jumped onto Ox's back.

Rat jumped on, too.

They held on tight.

All the animals were swimming fast.

Each one wanted to win the race.

Ox swam and swam.

Cat and Rat held onto his back.

"We are going to win!" shouted Cat.

"We are almost there," said Rat.

"Get ready to jump."

Cat was excited.

She and Rat were going to win the race

by cheating!

Ox swam closer and closer
to the river bank,
and Cat got ready to jump ...

Splash!

Suddenly, Cat was in the water.

Rat had pushed her in.

He had tricked her!

Cat did not like to swim.

She did not like the water.

She splashed and splashed

as she tried to swim to the river bank.

Ox swam on.

He reached the river bank first.

But Rat jumped off his back
and onto the land.

"I'm the winner!" shouted Rat.

"You cheated!" said Ox.

Rat came first.

Ox came second.

The Emperor named the first New Year

'The Year of the Rat'.

He named the next New Year

'The Year of the Ox'.

He named a New Year after the
next ten animals to finish the race.

But where was Cat?

At last, Cat reached the river bank.

She was very wet and very tired.

The Emperor shook his head at Cat.

"I am sorry," he said. "You are too late.

The first twelve animals

will have a New Year.

You are number thirteen.

There is no New Year left for you."

So, that is why there is no
Year of the Cat.
And that is why cats
are never friends with rats!

Story order

Look at these 5 pictures and captions.
Put the pictures in the right order
to retell the story.

Cat is about to win!

Cat falls into the water.

3

Cat crawls onto the riverbank.

4

The race begins!

5

Rat has a naughty plan.

Independent Reading

This series is designed to provide an opportunity for your child to read on their own. These notes are written for you to help your child choose a book and to read it independently.

In school, your child's teacher will often be using reading books which have been banded to support the process of learning to read. Use the book band colour your child is reading in school to help you make a good choice. *The Cat's Tale* is a good choice for children reading at Turquoise Band in their classroom to read independently.

The aim of independent reading is to read this book with ease, so that your child enjoys the story and relates it to their own experiences.

About the book

The Emperor wants to hold a race to decide which animals to name each year after. Cat does not like getting wet, but Rat has a plan and tells Cat they can swim on Ox's back. But Rat is going to cheat and pushes cat in!

Before reading

Help your child to learn how to make good choices by asking:

"Why did you choose this book? Why do you think you will enjoy it?"

Look at the cover together and ask: "What do you think the story will be about?" Ask your child to think of what they already know about the story context. Then ask your child to read the title aloud. Ask: "What do you know about cats in stories? What may show you that the story is set long ago?"

Remind your child that they can sound out the letters to make a word if they get stuck.

Decide together whether your child will read the story independently or read it aloud to you.

During reading

Remind your child of what they know and what they can do independently. If reading aloud, support your child if they hesitate or ask for help by telling the word. If reading to themselves, remind your child that they can come and ask for your help if stuck.

After reading

Support comprehension by asking your child to tell you about the story. Use the story order puzzle to encourage your child to retell the story in the right sequence, in their own words. The correct sequence can be found on the next page.

Help your child think about the messages in the book that go beyond the story and ask: "What lesson do you think Cat learned after the race?"

Give your child a chance to respond to the story: "Did you have a favourite part? Which animal did you want to win? Why?"

Extending learning

Help your child understand the story structure by using the same sentence patterning and adding different elements. "Let's make up a new story about how Rat wins a race. Where might the race be? What trick might he use? Who might help Rat?" Can you think of other traditonal tales about animals that you could alter, such as an Aesop's Fable or a Just So story?

In the classroom, your child's teacher may be teaching examples of descriptive language such as expressions about time. Locate the phrases relating to time in the story (such as 'long ago, 'after a while', 'suddenly' and 'at last'). Ask your child to find as many as they can, and then think of some more examples.

Franklin Watts
First published in Great Britain in 2018
by The Watts Publishing Group

Series Editors: Jackie Hamley and Melanie Palmer
Series Advisors: Dr Sue Bodman and Glen Franklin
Series Designer: Peter Scoulding

A CIP catalogue record for this book is
available from the British Library.

ISBN 978 1 4451 6179 2 (hbk)
ISBN 978 1 4451 6180 8 (pbk)
ISBN 978 1 4451 6181 5 (library ebook)

Printed in China

Franklin Watts
An imprint of
Hachette Children's Group
Part of The Watts Publishing Group
Carmelite House
50 Victoria Embankment
London EC4Y 0DZ

An Hachette UK Company
www.hachette.co.uk

www.franklinwatts.co.uk

Answer to Story order: 5, 4, 1, 2, 3